Woods,

ALL THE BEST!!

To Mother Nature for her inspiring creations ---- PJP

For Amy, Samantha and Sierra ---- MG

Tree Of Life Publishing
1001 Avenue of the Americas
12th Floor
New York NY 10018
www.treeoflifepublishing.com
www.peeperandfriends.com

Published by Peeper & Friends, an imprint of Tree Of Life Publishing 2004.

Printed in Hong Kong

Library of Congress Control Number: 2003096056

Library of Congress Cataloging-in-Publication Data
Parente, Peter, 1974-
Peeper the Kinkajou/by Peter Parente; illustrated by Michael Graham.
p. cm.

SUMMARY: A kinkajou learns about rainforest animals like sloths, tamanduas, marmosets, jaguars and anacondas while looking for new ways to entertain himself in the diminishing rainforest.

Audience: Grades 1-3.

1. Kinkajou--Juvenile fiction. 2. Rain forests--Juvenile fiction. [1. Kinkajou--Fiction. 2. Rain forest--Fiction. 3. Rain forest animals--Fiction.] I. Title.
PZ7.P2166Pe 2005   [E]   QBI05-220

ISBN 0-9745052-0-X

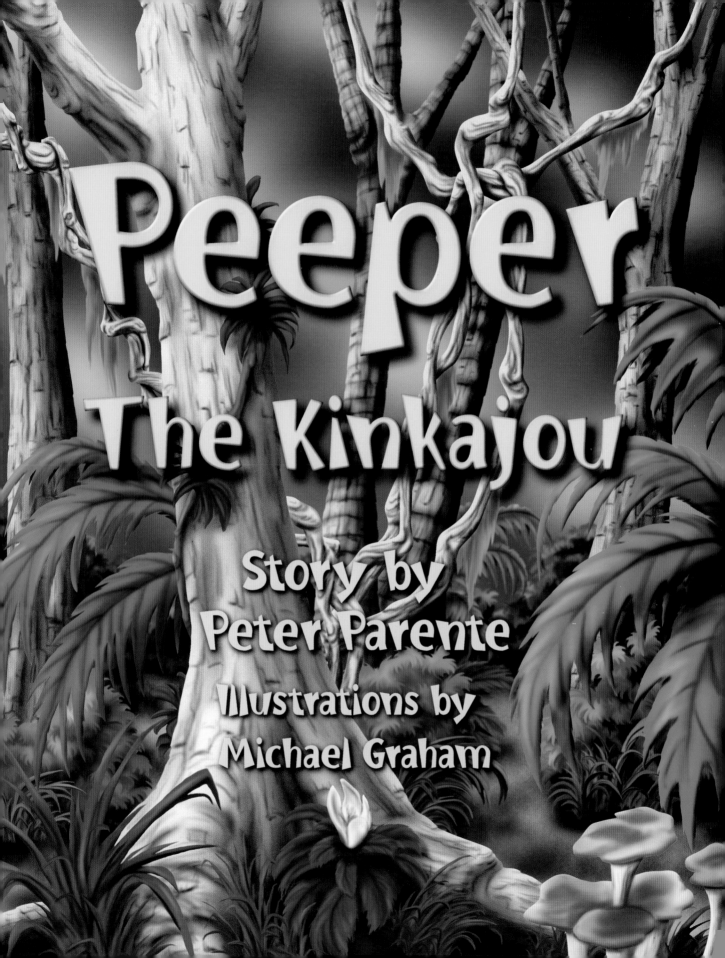

Peeper
The Kinkajou

Story by
Peter Parente

Illustrations by
Michael Graham

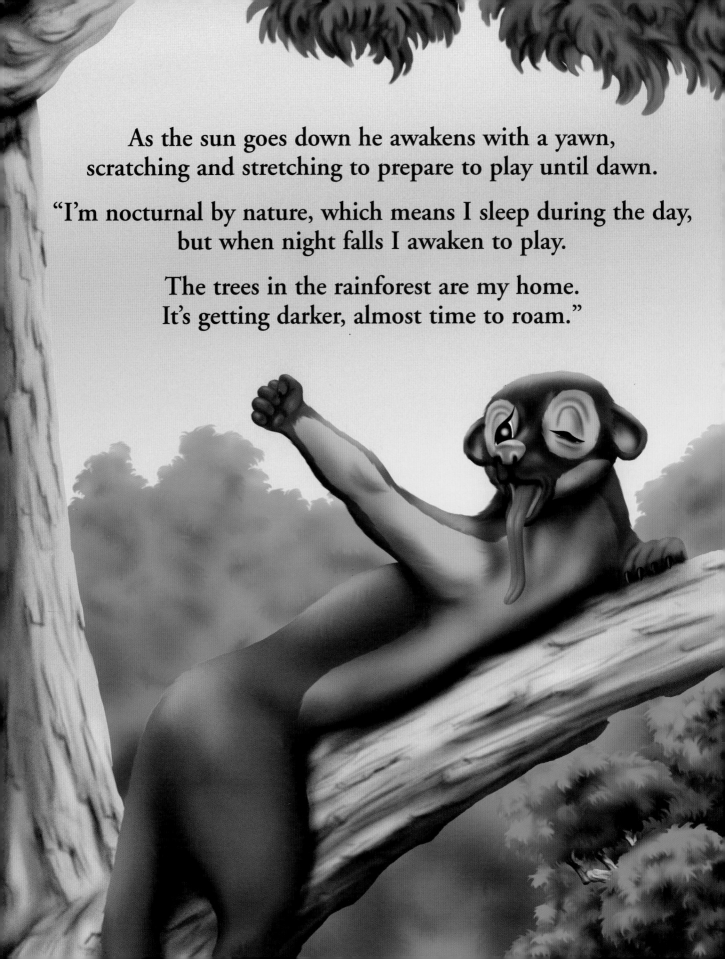

As the sun goes down he awakens with a yawn,
scratching and stretching to prepare to play until dawn.

"I'm nocturnal by nature, which means I sleep during the day,
but when night falls I awaken to play.

The trees in the rainforest are my home.
It's getting darker, almost time to roam."

"My name is Peeper because I can peep near or far.
I can peep loud enough for you to hear me wherever you are.

I have a long skinny tongue, ten fingers and toes,
a bright yellow belly, and a little pink nose.

My feet are like hands more than they are feet.
They can hold onto a branch or even a treat."

"My prehensile tail can be used for hanging around.
I'm usually in the trees, not on the ground.

I've eaten my fill of insects, fruit, and honey.
What else can I eat that will hit right on the money?

Shall I eat some eggs, leaves, or maybe a frog,
or I can use my long tongue to get nectar from the flowers on this log.

It looks like Kirby, the anteater, has been clawing
through some ant mounds.
He should slow down before he packs on any more pounds."

"Peeper, you missed the first three courses of beetles, termites, and ants.
Hang around while I give my long sticky tongue a rest and
loosen my pants.

Would you like to join me, I'm having fruit for dessert?
It's nice and sweet if you don't mind the dirt."

"No thank you, Kirby, I was just looking around.
I dropped down to see who was making all the noise on the ground."

"I can wake up Maggie, the two-toed sloth, with a peep.
She has already had twenty hours of sleep.

She may be hard of hearing and doesn't have the best eyesight,
but a good sense of smell helps her at night."

"Hello Peeper," Maggie said with a smile.
"Have I been sleeping for a while?"

"It's been a full day since you climbed in the sack.
It's been so long blue-green algae has grown on your back."

"The algae helps me camouflage myself in the tree
and I move too slowly for anyone to spot me."

"Do you have any big plans for the night
or are you going to lay low and hang out of sight?"

"I think I'll take a few hours to travel to the branch next door.
I smell some tasty leaves that I just can't ignore."

"I always get tired when I hang out with you.
I'm going to get sleepy if I don't find something else to do."

"Hello Peeper, how are you today?
I'm hungry. I mean bored. Would you like to come
down and play?

The best climbers of all cats are jaguars like me.
If you prefer to stay there I can climb up the tree."

"Jaguars have big teeth and powerful claws.
If I get too close I may become trapped in those jaws."

"Sorry Sheeba, I have to be on my way
or else I would love to come down and play.

I'll go and find Oliver, Frankie and Lou.
Those crazy marmosets always have something fun to do."

"You all better stop monkeying around
or Sheeba might get you if you fall to the ground."

"A marmoset may be the smallest monkey you will ever see,
but I can move so quickly she could not catch me."

"We can move up and down, left or right,
so quickly, in a flash, we're out of your sight.

We are playing human in the middle, if you want to stay.
We only have a few hours until the light of day."

"I'll leave you to the game that you play every night
to make one more stop before the first light.

I can find Sam, the green anaconda, who is twenty-seven feet in size.
He may not be cute and cuddly, but he is very wise."

"I knew this tree on the river bank was where you would be,
waiting to drop in on a meal just like me."

"A meal is something I would never consider you at all.
You would be more like an appetizer being so small."

"Ever since man started cutting down our home,
each day there is less land where we can all roam.

I have been trying to figure out something different to do.
I came to see if you might have a clue."

"The tarpon, also known as the Silver King, migrate each year.
In spring they go to Florida and in fall they come back here."

"That's it! A vacation to a far off land.
Florida has palm trees and beautiful sand.

Thank you for giving me that wonderful tip.
I'll be sure to get you a souvenir when I go on my trip."

Peeper went back home to his branch on his tree
to get some rest for his magnificent journey.

As the sun started to shine he laid down for the day
for when night falls again he will be on his way.

Aviarios del Caribe
Sloth Rescue Center

When the 1991 earthquake shook their home to the ground, Judy and Luis Arroyo rebuilt it as a Bed & Breakfast. They offered tours of their jungle and island, showcasing over 300 bird species. Their destiny changed when 3 neighbor girls brought them a wee surprise, an orphaned three-toed sloth. They named her Buttercup. Finding scant literature on sloths, they learned from experience. Then another sloth arrived. And another. Before long the Arroyos became known as authorities on sloth rescue and rearing. The sloths kept coming. Buttercup became the most loved and photographed sloth in the world.

In 1998 the Arroyos gave into the sloths. They had their island designated a Nation Preserve, and opened the Aviarios Sloth Rescue Center. In addition to rehabilitating and caring for sloths, they care for every animal that needs to be attended to. They have successfully reintroduced two hand-reared orphans into the rainforest. Dozens of sloths that arrived at the center as adults have been rehabilitated and returned to the forest canopy as well.

The Rescue Center teaches Costa Rican children to appreciate sloths and their forest ecosystem, and provides a clearing house for information and techniques of sloth care and rearing. As species are pushed ever closer to the brink, this knowledge is critical.

Future plans for the Rescue Center include an international veterinary study station, partnership with jungle researchers worldwide, and purchase of the remainder of the island to complete the Refuge. All this costs money; a great deal of money, which the Arroyos are supplying through their tourism activities. The sloths need more than what Judy and Luis can provide. They need your help. Consider adopting a sloth (or two!), or a bequest for one of their major projects. The Rescue Center is a U.S. 501 (c)3, so all contributions are tax-deductible. The sloths thank you-slowly, quietly, but most sincerely. For additional information on adoptions you can contact Peeper & Friends.

www.slothrescue.org
aviarios@costarica.net
P.O. Box 569-7300, Limon, Costa Rica, C.A.
(011-506)750-0775